A Summery Saturday Morning

To Alice and Poppy –
the goose-and-dog girls, M.M.

For my mum, S.Y.

PUFFIN BOOKS

Published by the Penguin Group
Penguin Group (NZ), 67 Apollo Drive, Rosedale,
North Shore 0632, New Zealand (a division of Pearson New Zealand Ltd)
Penguin Group (USA) Inc., 375 Hudson Street,
New York, New York 10014, USA
Penguin Group (Canada), 90 Eglinton Avenue East, Suite 700, Toronto,
Ontario, M4P 2Y3, Canada (a division of Pearson Penguin Canada Inc.)
Penguin Books Ltd, 80 Strand, London, WC2R 0RL, England
Penguin Ireland, 25 St Stephen's Green,
Dublin 2, Ireland (a division of Penguin Books Ltd)
Penguin Group (Australia), 250 Camberwell Road, Camberwell,
Victoria 3124, Australia (a division of Pearson Australia Group Pty Ltd)
Penguin Books India Pvt Ltd, 11, Community Centre,
Panchsheel Park, New Delhi – 110 017, India
Penguin Books (South Africa) (Pty) Ltd, 24 Sturdee Avenue,
Rosebank, Johannesburg 2196, South Africa

Penguin Books Ltd, Registered Offices: 80 Strand, London, WC2R 0RL, England

First published by Hamish Hamilton Ltd, Great Britain, 1998
Published in Puffin Books, 1999
This edition published in Puffin Books, 2010

10 9 8

Copyright © Margaret Mahy, 1998
Illustrations © Selina Young, 1998

The right of Margaret Mahy to be identified as the author of this work in terms of
section 96 of the Copyright Act 1994 is hereby asserted.

Designed by Book Design Ltd www.bookdesign.co.nz
Printed in China through APOL, Hong Kong

ISBN: 9 78 0 14350452 8

A catalogue record for this book is available
from the National Library of New Zealand.

www.penguin.co.nz

A Summery Saturday Morning

Written by Margaret Mahy

Illustrated by Selina Young

PUFFIN BOOKS

We take the dogs down the wiggly track,
The wiggly track, the wiggly track.
One dog's white and the other dog's black
On a summery Saturday morning.

Bad dogs, bad dogs chase the cat,
Chase the cat, chase the cat.
One dog's thin and the other dog's fat
On a summery Saturday morning.

They chase the boy on the rattly bike,
The rattly bike, the rattly bike.
Chasing things is what dogs like
On a summery Saturday morning.

Long grass grows on the edge of the sea,
The edge of the sea, the edge of the sea.
The wind is blowing wild and free
On a summery Saturday morning.

A goose looks out of the tangled green,
The tangled green, the tangled green.
Her neck is long and her eye is mean
On a summery Saturday morning.

Another goose . . . and then another,
Then another, then another!
Seven sleek sisters out with mother
On a summery Saturday morning.

The geese begin to run away,
Run away, run away.
The dogs run, too. They want to play
On a summery Saturday morning.

We run, too, to catch the dogs,
To catch the dogs, to catch the dogs.
Scattering shells and leaping logs
On a summery Saturday morning.

The mud begins its guggliwugs,
Its guggliwugs, its guggliwugs.
Our sandals slide like slugliwugs
On a summery Saturday morning.

The geese turn round and flap and hiss,
Flap and hiss, flap and hiss.
The dogs were not expecting this
On a summery Saturday morning.

The geese begin to chase us back,
To chase us back, to chase us back.
Out of the mud and up the track
On a summery Saturday morning.

If you want to walk in peace,
Walk in peace, walk in peace,
Don't let your dogs upset the geese
On a summery Saturday morning.